Monkey Belle's
DREAM

Written by Didi McKay

Illustrated by Jaz Richardson

Balboa Press books may be ordered through booksellers or by contacting:

Balboa Press
A Division of Hay House
1663 Liberty Drive
Bloomington, IN 47403
www.balboapress.com
844-682-1282

Because of the dynamic nature of the Internet, any web addresses or links contained in this book may have changed since publication and may no longer be valid. The views expressed in this work are solely those of the author and do not necessarily reflect the views of the publisher, and the publisher hereby disclaims any responsibility for them.

ISBN: 978-1-9822-5805-4 (sc)
ISBN: 978-1-9822-5807-8 (hc)
ISBN: 978-1-9822-5806-1 (e)

Library of Congress Control Number: 2020921802

Print information available on the last page.

Balboa Press rev. date: 11/03/2020

BALBOA.PRESS
A DIVISION OF HAY HOUSE

**With much appreciation, thank you to my editor
Pamela Preston for her patience and heart.**

**A huge, happy thank you to the following supporters
who helped bring Monkey Belle's Dream to life:**

Wiley McKay Conte

Liz Rogers Stone

Doug Ryan

David Jenkins

David Wald

Mark Ryan

Bob Conte and Kristina Lindbergh

Jace and Jaxx Maggi

Sally and Dan Breen

H. Michael Heuser, Grandad of Willa and Nina

Harriet Tolve for her grandchildren

Addison and Thomas

Anne L. McKay

John Cotton McKay

Nancy McKay and Mia S. McKay

Bill, Maryann Dixon and Randolph Cotton McKay

Sunny Utz

Cyndi Flanagan

Lois Lavelle

Jeni Spaeth

Andi Bovarnick

Linda Parker

Gina Brulato

Cheri Killian, Roxi and fur babies

Ilse Soar, Tressa's Omi

Cathy

Mare Schelz

Melody Somogyi

King and Amsterdam Gumatay

Leslie MacKimm McCarthy

Nancy Benerofe

Sujatha Raman

Hyla Crane

Michelle Sager

Cheryl Sokolow

Introduction

Imagine: Monkey Belle's Dream can be a playful springboard for exploring sleep, dreams, art and language. In the role of children's first teachers, parents can use encouraging tools such as smiles, questions, listening, patience and pauses.

Keep a pen and designated notebook handy to jot down the child's own poem or story.

When children have a colorful purpose or vision for their penmanship and wordsmithing, it's fun! Support them with space and time to illustrate or act out their own sweet dreams or fantastic worlds, complete with props, costumes, songs or dance.

Ask: There's magic in the doing, so try out some experiential or inquiry-based learning. When the experience of reading Monkey Belle's Dream is interactive, children's curiosity and questioning will naturally arise, so allow time for reflection, observation and laughs! For example, ask children what they think happens when they close their eyes and fall asleep. What will their dream look and feel like when it includes things they love, like unicorns or puppies, puddles or swings?

Simply inquire, "What would you like to dream about tonight?" Perhaps they have a problem to solve such as finding a lost item or sharing their toys. Quietly listen to their comments, questions and responses.

Try peeking back and forward through the pages. Look together through the story to find items from Monkey Belle's bedroom that appear in her dream.

Creation Station: Have children envision and draw their own magical dreamscapes where anything is possible.

Set up a comfortable creation space that fits the child's preferences. Do they like to stretch out on the floor or instead be outside under a shady tree? Do they prefer silence or music? The sounds of birds or their own singing? Even the kitchen sink and some water can be a place where imaginations flow. Ask them if they like clay, crayons, or sparkly pens and cut paper. Then spark your child with the question, "What will you make today?"

Hands-on creating will build your child's fine motor skills and hand-eye coordination and can be a great tool for unwinding, self-soothing and calming. Have them participate in fashioning their own creation station or cozy, book-time and bedtime spaces or routines. Encourage their imaginations and organization skills by letting them try things by themselves. Have fun!

Monkey Belle's Dream

On a high, green hill
Up a tall, bushy tree
Lived one little Monkey Belle
With her parents made three.

While Monkey Belle slept
She dreamed a sweet dream

Of swirly, red lollies
And puffy, nut cream.

She dreamed that she floated
Down a sparkly soda stream

In a chocolate brown boat
With a sail of apple-green.

In the foamy, funny water
She spied some gummy fish
That were pink and yellow-spotted
And they swam with a swish!

Eating sweets made Belle thirsty
So she dreamed a blue lake

Crystal clear to the bottom
Around a mountain-sized cake.

Monkey Belle soon remembered
As she dozed in her dream
That she forgot to brush her teeth
To keep them shiny clean.

So she rose from her slumber
And she stepped from her bed

Still lost in thoughts of fruity shapes
Swimming in her head.

Monkey Belle found her toothbrush
And she brushed up her teeth

Then she dazedly crept back to bed
And smiled herself to sleep.

About the Author:

Didi (Deirdre) McKay is an artist, writer, wellness advocate and mom to Wiley and Isabel (Ellie Belle), who inspired this story. Didi has developed and taught hundreds of children's and wellness programs and activities in museums, art centers, libraries, summer camps and schools. She loves creating and is an empowerment coach to other imaginative women.

You'll find many of Didi's children's childhood treasures such as Ellie's "pinky" blanket, art supplies, and pet dog on the pages of Monkey Belle's Dream. Didi's other books include *Gifts of the Trees, Gifts of the Seas,* and *Gifts of the Animals,* a series promoting gratitude and cultural understanding.

You can find Didi's creations on FB at Didi Designs: https://www.facebook.com/artblissed and Instagram: https://www.instagram.com/didi_siri_art/

About the Illustrator:

Jaz is a fun and loving person who is easy to get along with. He spent most of his childhood in what he describes as "the middle of nowhere" New York, running around in fields and making up stories in his head. From made-up creatures to alternate worlds, Jaz now brings these stories to life and also enjoys illustrating the tales of others to share with the world.

You can see his work at: www.jazmenrichardson.com

Printed in the United States
By Bookmasters